A mouse, a frog, a snail, and a sparrow decide to find out. But as each animal announces their daring feat, a naysayer

First published in the United States, Great Britain, Canada, Australia, and New Zealand in 2014
by North-South Books Inc., an imprint of Nord-Süd Verlag AG, CH-8005, Zürich, Switzerland.

Distributed in the United States by North-South Books Inc., New York 10016.
Library of Congress Cataloging-in-Publication Data is available.

ISBN: 978-0-7358-4182-6
Printed in China by Leo Paper Products Ltd.,
Heshan, Guangdong, April 2014.
1 3 5 7 9 • 10 8 6 4 2

www.northsouth.com

FSC
www.fsc.org
MIX
Paper from
responsible sources
FSC® C020056

You Call That Brave?

Lorenz Pauli • Kathrin Schärer

North
South

The mouse, the snail, the frog, and the sparrow sat by the side of the pond. The mouse was there because she didn't know where else to go. The snail was there because the mouse was there. The frog just happened to have hopped in that direction . . .

. . . and the sparrow wanted to know what the others were doing there.

"What *are* we doing here?" asked the mouse.

"That's a good question," said the snail.

"So what are we *going* to do?" asked the sparrow.

The others shook their heads and tried to think of what to do.

It was the frog who finally came up with an answer. "Let's have a competition to see which of us is the bravest."

"Good idea!"
"Great idea!"
"Super idea!"
The others all clapped their paws, wings, or antennae.

The mouse went first.

"I will swim underwater to the other side of the pond and back again without coming up for air!"

The frog made a face. "Hokey-crokey, you call that being brave? That's just having fun!"

The mouse was very offended. "I'm not a frog. What's fun for you is a fearsome feat for me!"

"Okay, okay," said the sparrow, trying to calm things down. "Show us what you can do."

The mouse got ready. She took a deep breath, dove into the water, and away she went.

All the way there, all the way back.

At last the mouse emerged from the pond. She was puffing and panting.

The frog helped her out of the water and congratulated her. "Bravo, brave mouse. You're a great swimmer."

And they all clapped their webbed feet, antennae, or wings.

Now it was the frog's turn.

"Today I'm not going to eat any silly spiders or flashy flies," he said. "I'm going to eat a whole, great big water lily!"

The snail made a face. "Slithery-slide, you call that being brave? I eat green stuff all day long."

"Maybe you do," said the frog, who was very offended. "But I'm a frog, and eating greens is breathtakingly brave."

"Okay, okay," said the mouse, trying to calm things down. "Go on, frog, show us what you can do."

The frog jumped into the pond, picked out a large water lily, and . . .

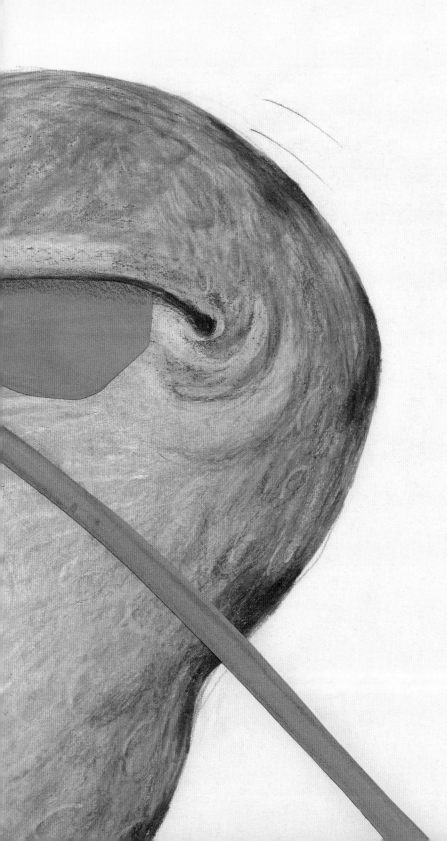

. . . swallowed it from stamen to stalk.

After the last gulp, the snail nodded her head in recognition of the frog's courage. "Bravo, brave frog! That was really something special."

And they all clapped their paws, wings, or antennae.

Now it was the snail's turn.

She slid here, and slithered there, cleared her throat, and said, "I am now going to creep out of my house, crawl all the way around it, and then go back inside."

The sparrow made a face. "Cheepy-chirp, you call that being brave? I left my eggshell on the day I was born, and I've never ever gone back inside!"

The snail, who was very offended, retreated into her shell.

"Okay, okay," said the mouse, trying to calm things down. "An eggshell is not a snail shell, so come on, snail, show us what you can do."

The snail crawled all the way out of her shell, crept all around her house . . .

. . . and then very, very slowly squeezed back inside. Now the house
was a little bit crooked.

The sparrow was very impressed. "Bravo, brave snail. No one's ever seen anything like that before!"
And they all clapped their wings, webbed feet, or paws.

Now they all looked with great excitement at the sparrow. Because everyone knows that sparrows are very bold and very brave.

They all waited eagerly to see what the sparrow would do. The sparrow stepped here, strode there, and strutted everywhere. . . .

At last the mouse understood. Then the frog understood.
And finally the snail understood.

And all of them shouted at once: **"Yes, that's how to be brave!"**